haiu-qt seared

harry k stammer

Sandy Press

haiu-qt seared

harry k stammer

Cover design, cover preparation, & interior layout by harry k stammer

ISBN: 979-8-9924582-7-5

Printed in U.S.A.

Sandy Press
Sandy-press.com

Some of the pieces have appeared in *Scud, dadakuku, and Synchronized Chaos. Thanks to the editors.*

scratch scratch scratch scratch scratch

Table of Contents

haiu-qt seared #23

{ k a ::)
t a l - l k r
(:: a k }

haiu-qt seared #22

g d t m t
h e s n s q
i f t m t

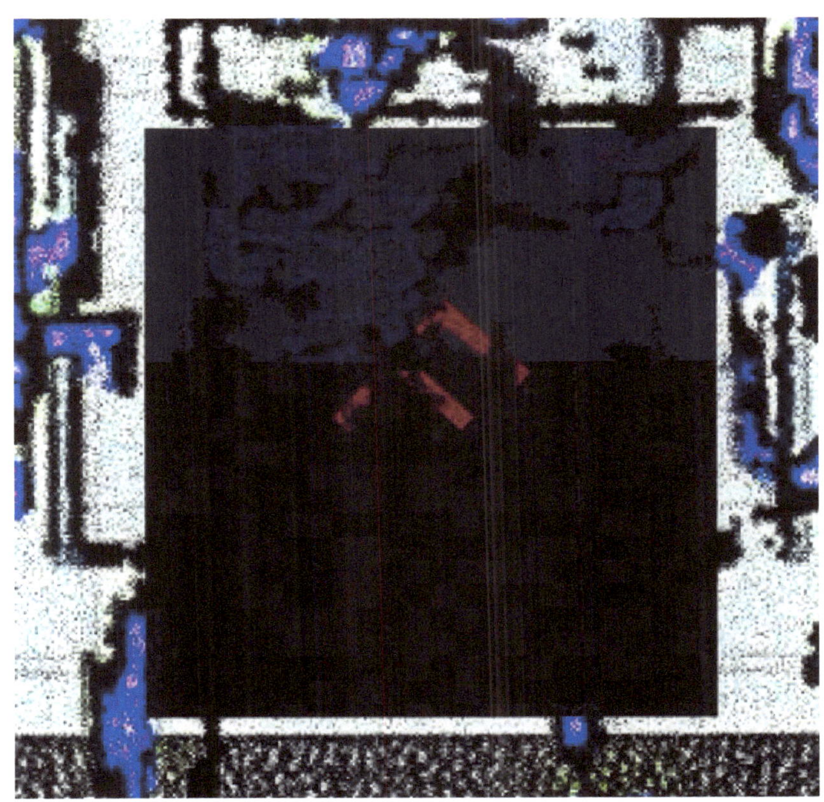

haiu-qt seared #21

p m t w i

a q r t s p b

o n s x h

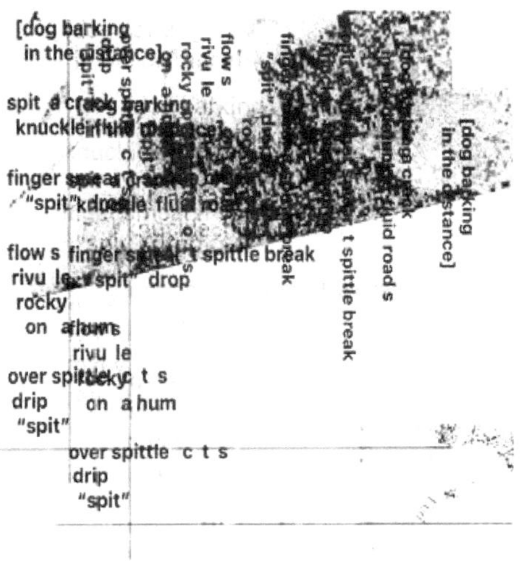

[dog barking
in the distance]
spit a crack barking
knuckle flu
finger sp   cracking
"spit" knuckle flu   ro
flow s finger sp   t spittle break
rivu le spit   drop
rocky
on a hum
rivu le
over spittle   c t s
drip
"spit"
over spittle c t s
drip
"spit"
[dog barking
in the distance]
t spittle break
liquid road s
flow s
rivu le
rocky

haiu-qt seared #20

L c 2 F g
r v m g K c 4
g 3 d E M

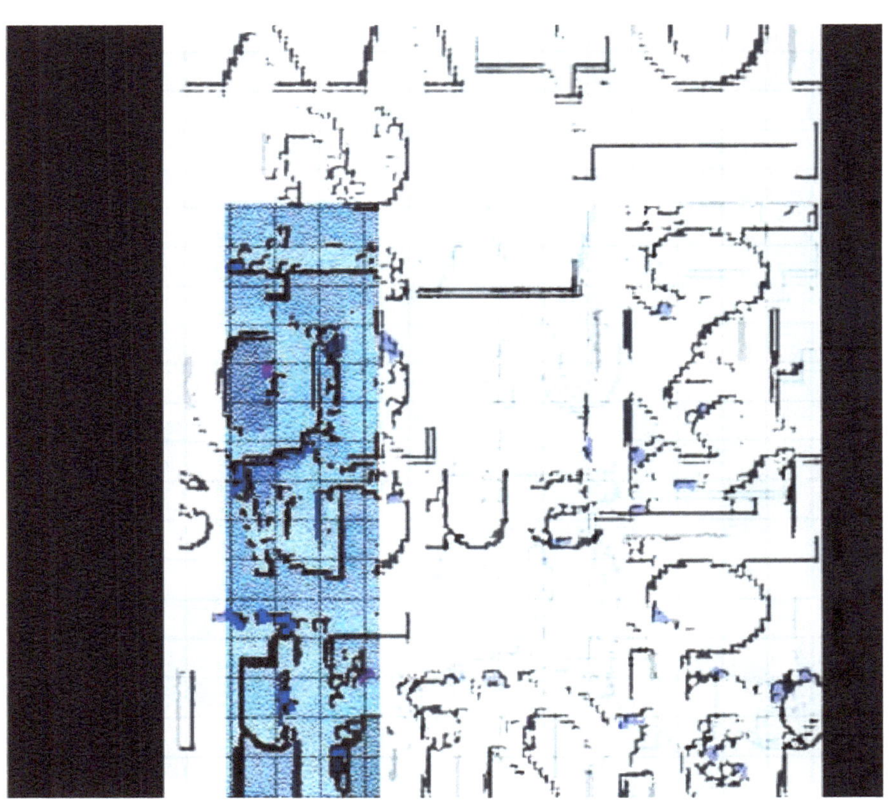

haiu-qt seared #19

q p t r e

r o s u f o s

f g h i j

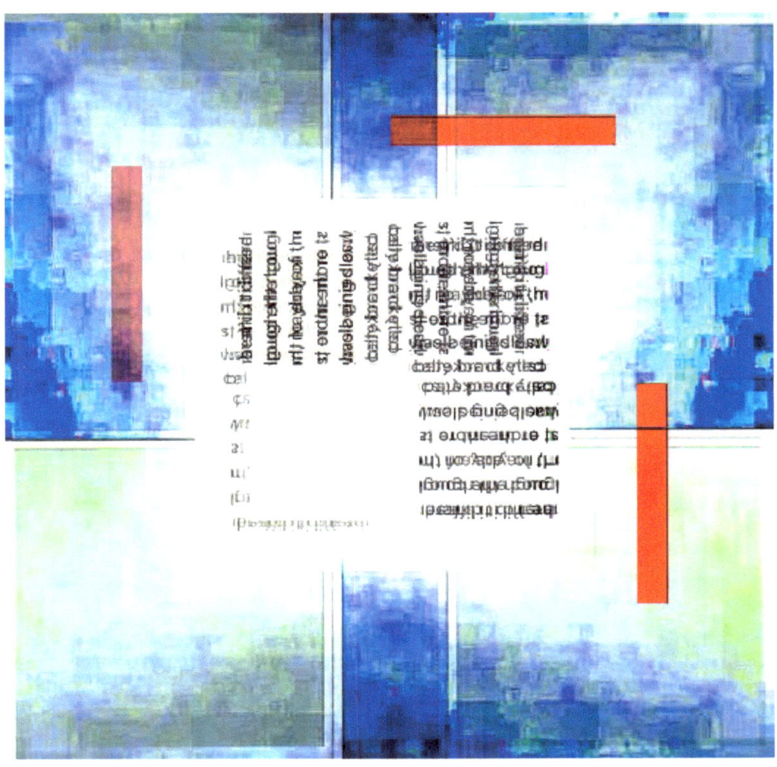

haiu-qt seared #18

: r : g :
; b ; d ; z :
: r : g :

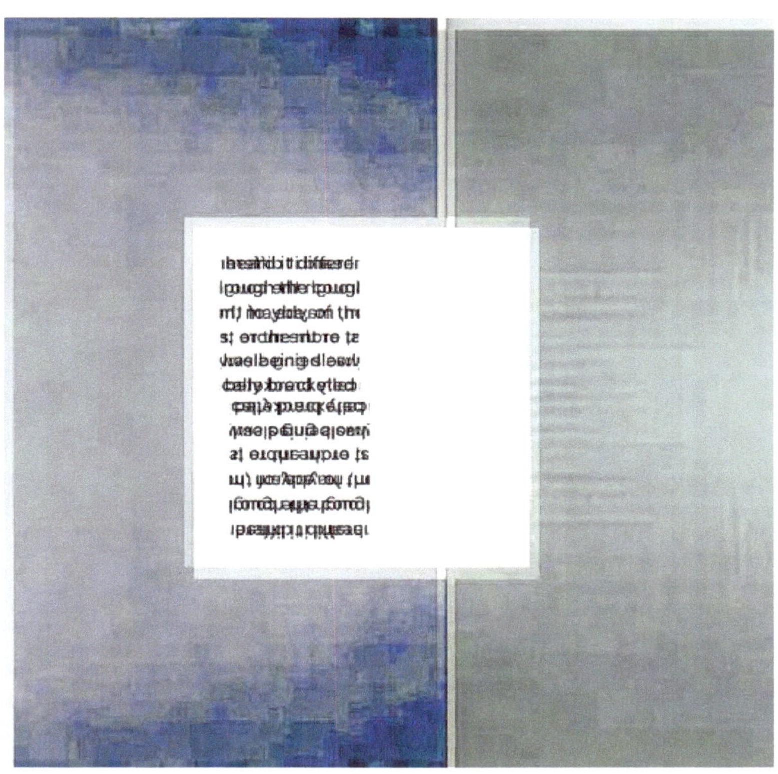

haiu-qt seared #17

p a y E w
B u g p t r s
d e T r s

haiu-qt seared #16

p i c k d

p e p p e r s

p i c k l

haiu-qt seared #15

p i c k l

p e p p e r s

p i c k d

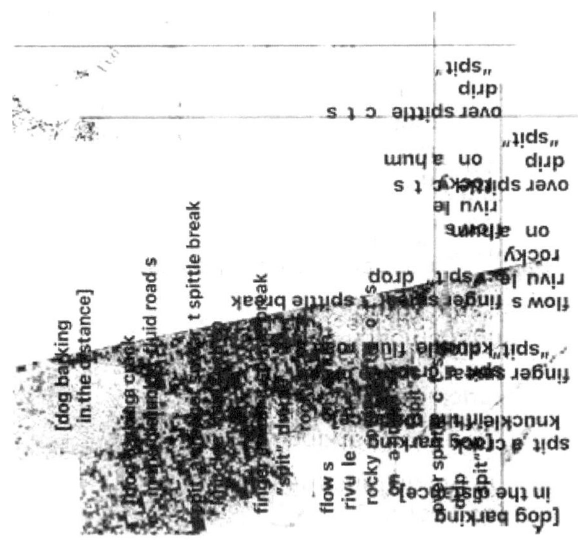
[dog barking
in the distance]
spit a c dog barking
knuckle flin
finger s
flow s finger s t spittle break
rivu le
rocky
on a hum
over spittle c t s
drip
"spit"
t spittle break
liquid road s
over spittle c t s
drip
"spit"

haiu-qt seared #14

tearp

ugainst

tearp

t spittle break
a spittle break
qsbpjpbfg
fluid road s

haiu-qt seared #13

p a r k i t
d a v c m d n
p a r k i t

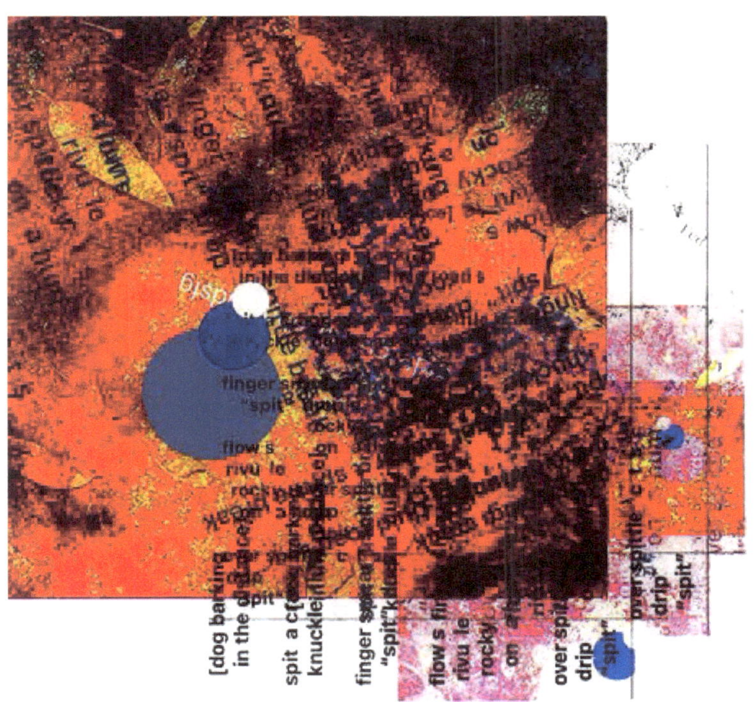
[dog barking
in the d...
spit a c[
knuckle
finger sp...
"spit"
flow s fi
rivu le
rocky
on a
over spit
drip
"spit"

haiu-qt seared #12

b r a r t

s w o c h e r

i n g h b

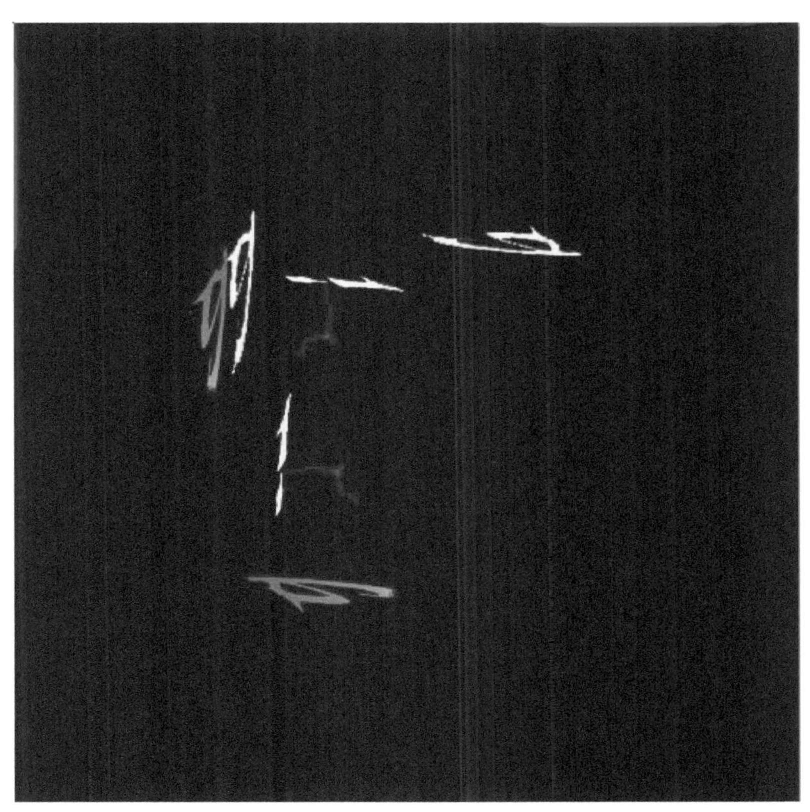

haiu-qt seared #11

k p t d i
M v / ^ > t e
i d t p k

RQEHIPCSJH
RQEHIPCSJH

haiu-qt seared #10

p y f h j

c t w e u x

o x g i k

haiu-qt seared #9

d w p q m

o P x e r t b

v a t i q

haiu-qt seared #8

p t e r n

o b r n o p e

n r e t p

roc k bord er t wi~th loßse   grav el
s'[bub blin g] d o~ut   ro~cky here
 "her e" scramb-led   it
boo t s giv e s'[bub blin g]

haiu-qt seared #7

m n p q r
m n o p q r t
m n p q r

haiu-qt seared #6

p r p l et
h n g y 2 d a
p r p l es

haiu-qt seared #5

0 i t 8 j k s

c 1 2 x c

f 0 3 m p s z

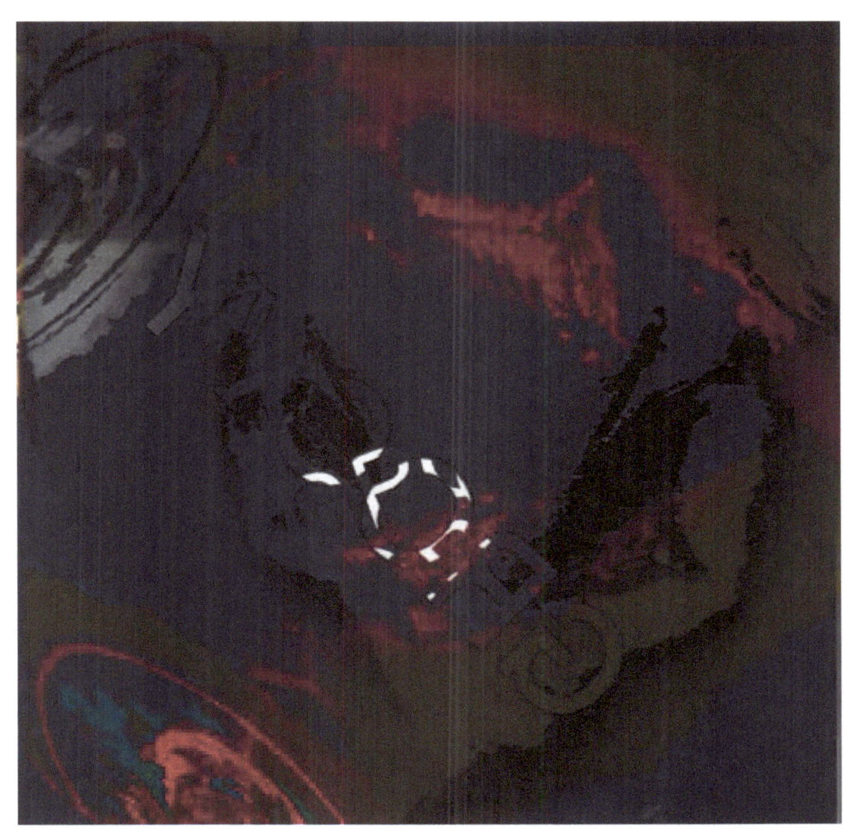

haiu-qt seared #4

s q a x n O o
d w X m U
s q a x o O m

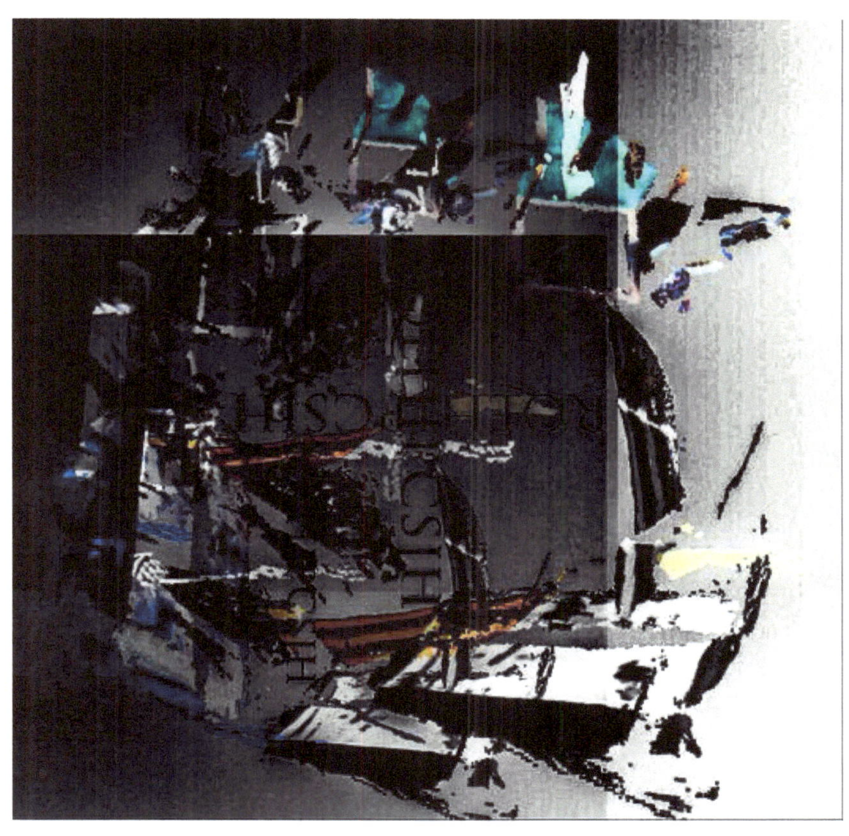

haiu-qt seared #3

s q t e k

d h i r e o n

z k t y s

haiu-qt seared #2

8 (n s 4

r R ! b y p o

a t o e u

pale
s

haiu-qt seared #1

d q u i t

a w o e l h r

s q t r t

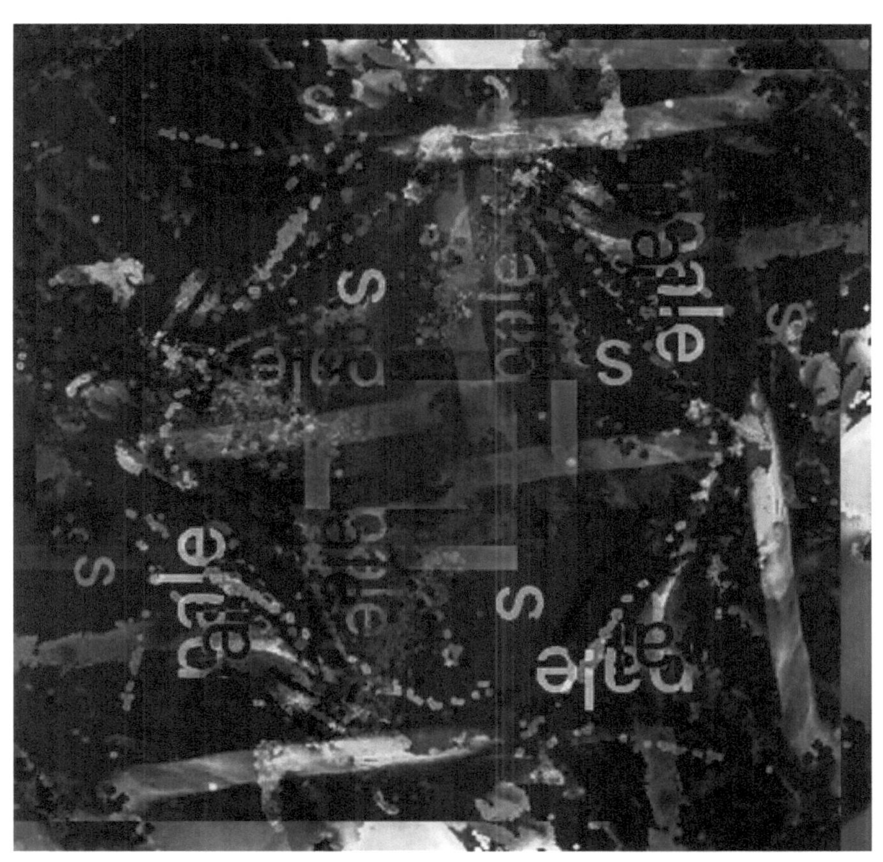

sale
sale
sale
sale
sale

haiu-qt seared #44

s k i e t

// f // h // j m

t l e f s

haiu-qt seared #43

s y , s w
p : p f p f p
a r t y f

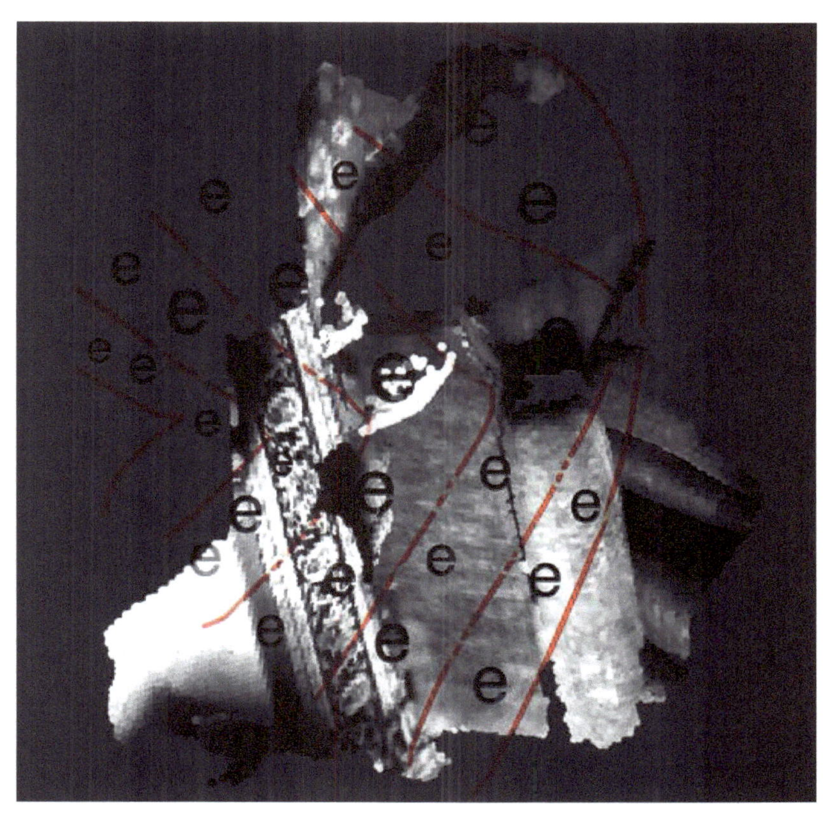

haiu-qt seared #42

: : d : d

: : : d : d :

d : d : :

haiu-qt seared #41

s j t q m
" " " f ' ' '
t k s r n

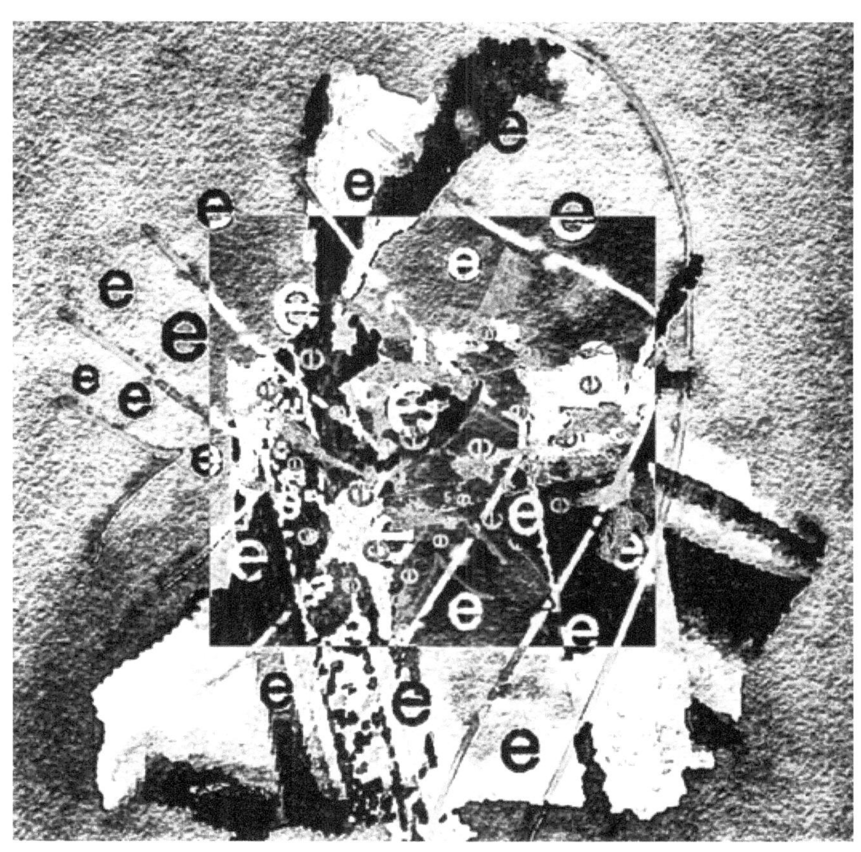

haiu-qt seared #40

p y e q a

i g s n t c p

o x f r b

haiu-qt seared #39

t k m f u

s t h e t p s

s l n g o

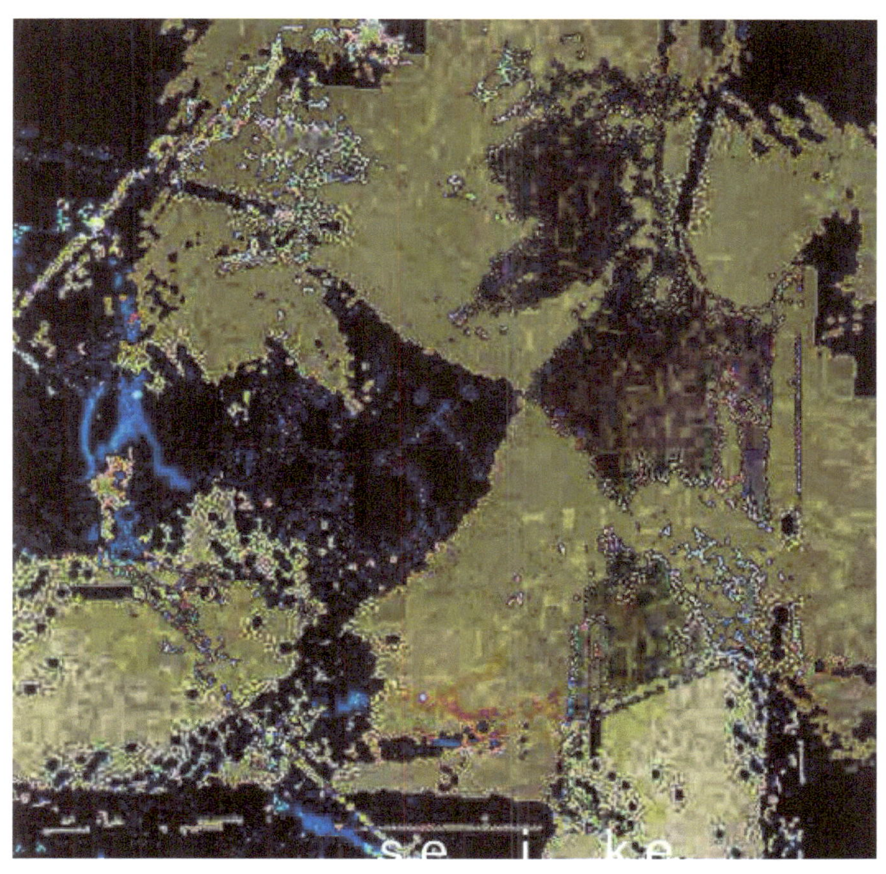

se i ke

haiu-qt seared #38

z j y e q
a M c t a n o
a k z f r

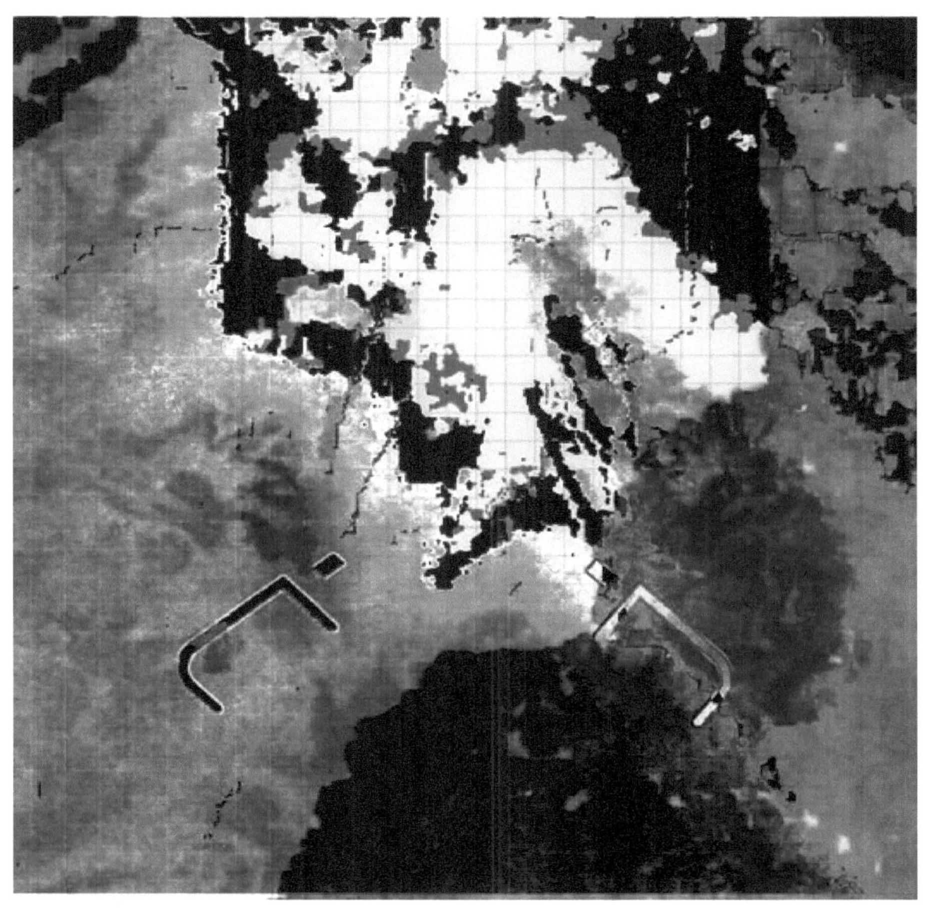

haiu-qt seared #37

s q z e e
t (y) r r s
f f a r t

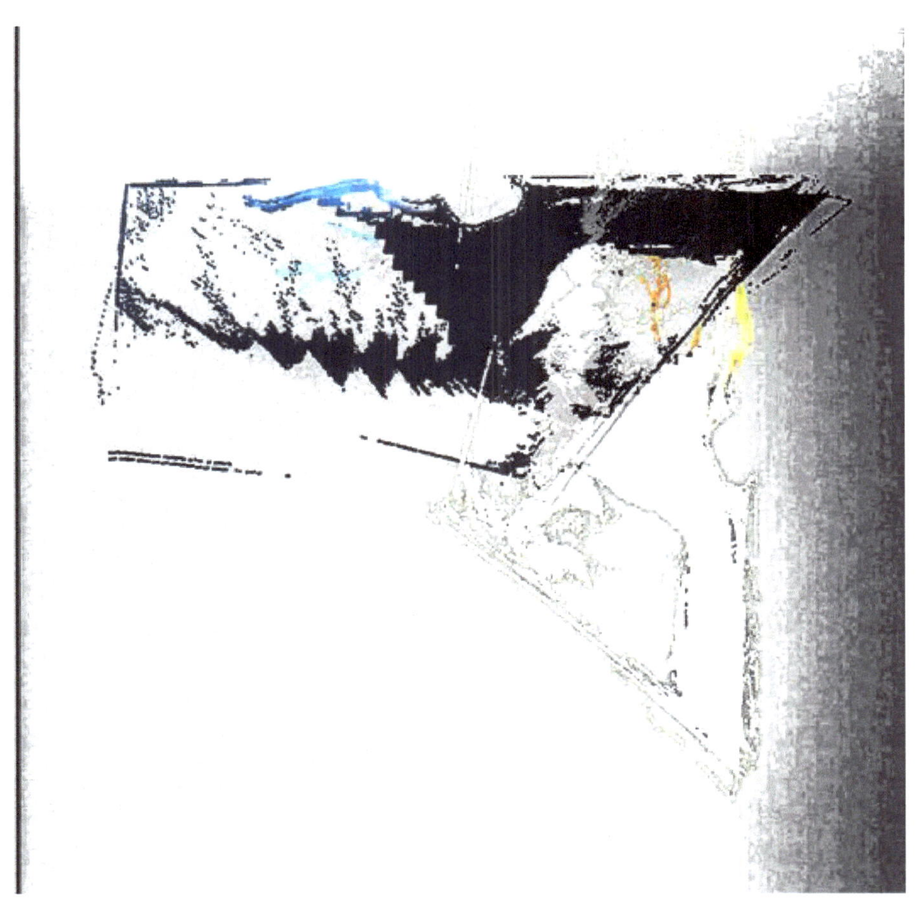

haiu-qt seared #36

s n u t a

f 0 h o r e r

t m y x b

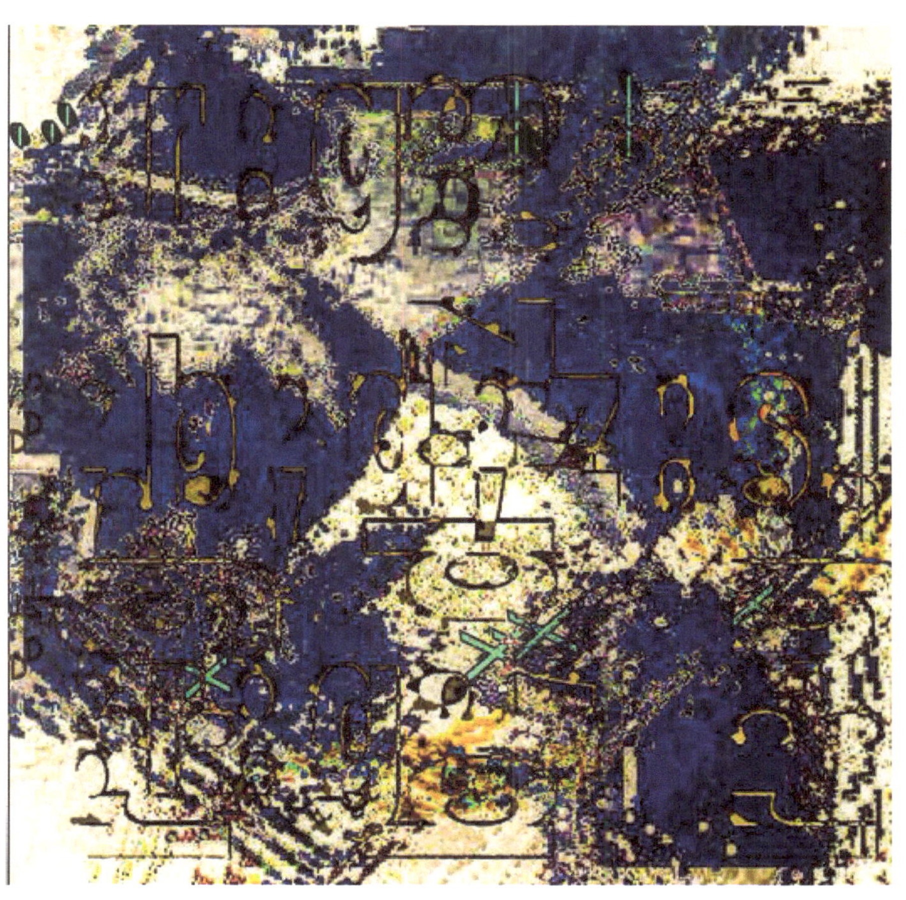

haiu-qt seared #35

p e R s n

f d S t m o n

q f T t n

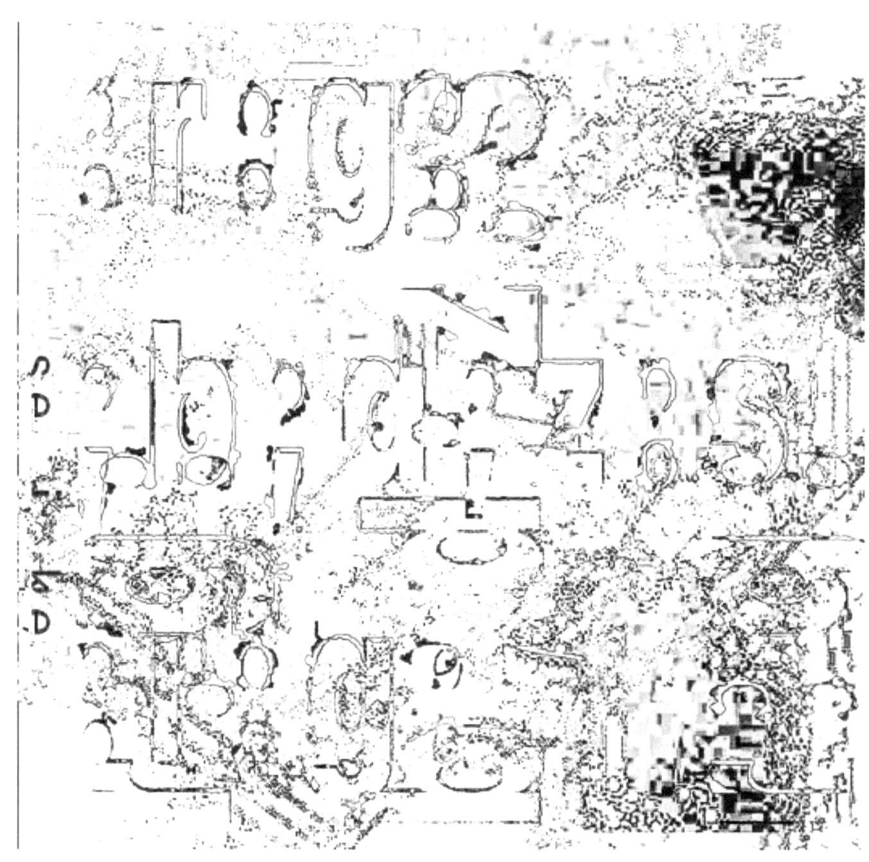

haiu-qt seared #34

c o c k d
b $ f o t a s
d p d l e

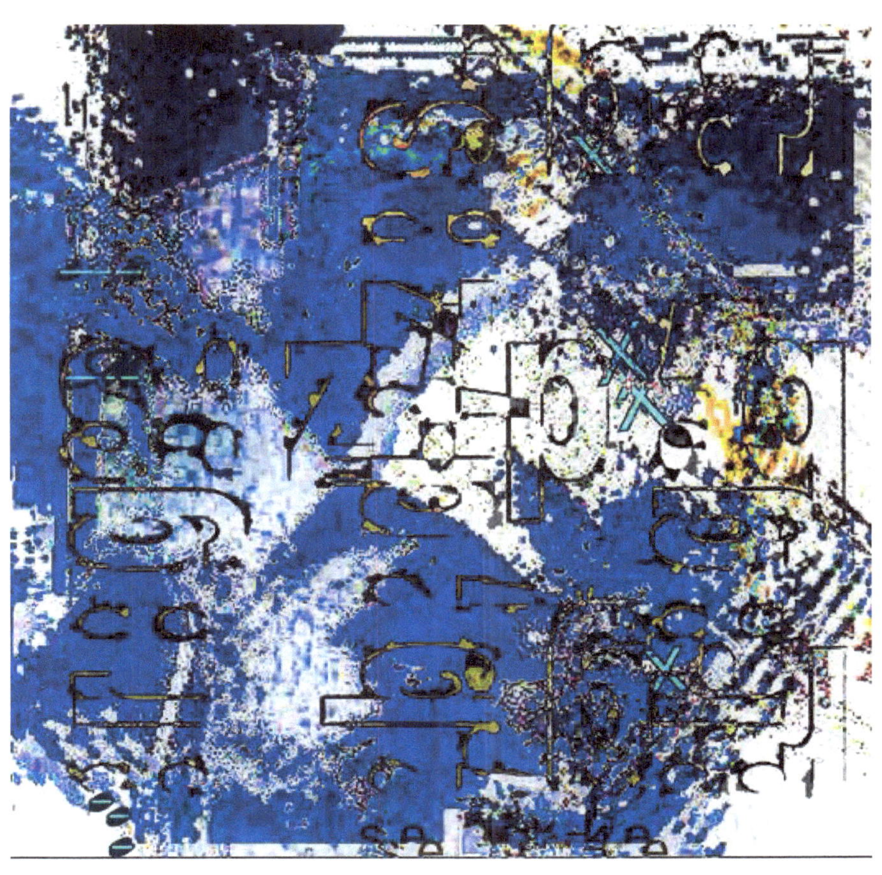

haiu-qt seared #33

? Y d f g
a E 8 ; f i g
 ! Z e g h

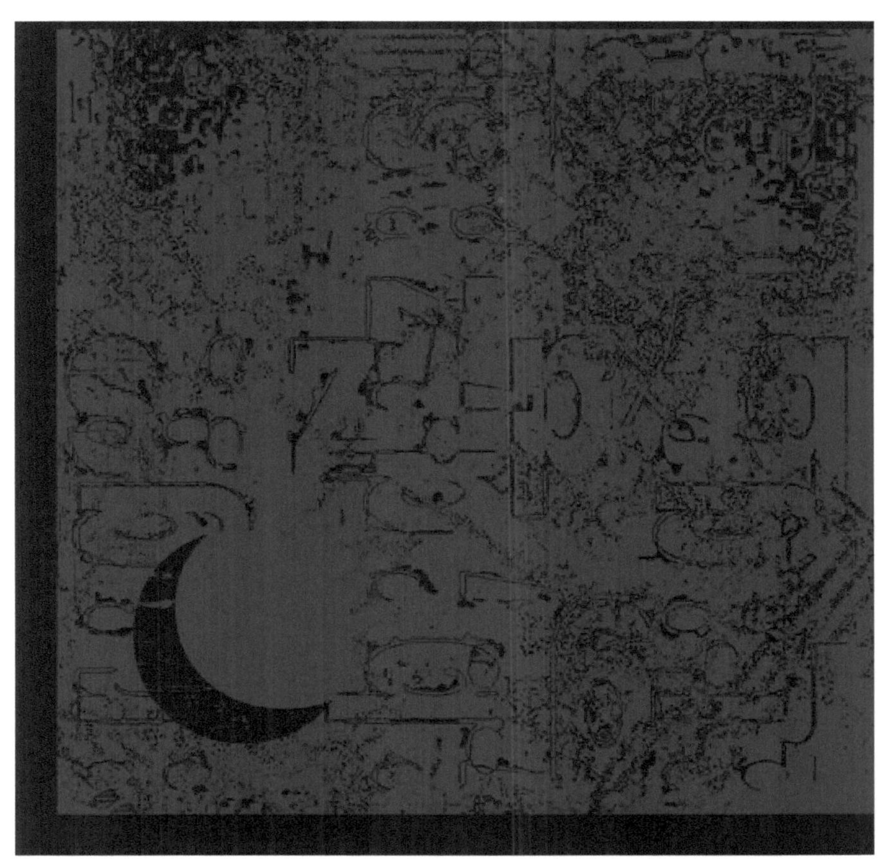

haiu-qt seared #32

b s t o p

s q u o n d r

c t o p q

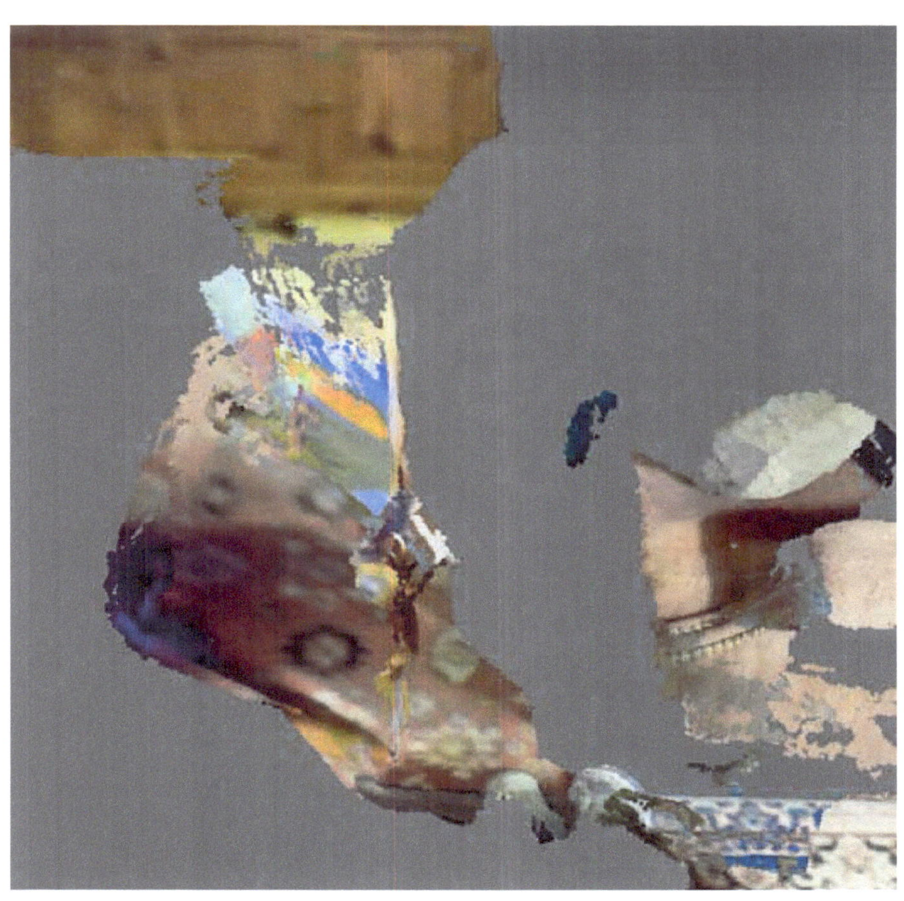

haiu-qt seared #31

z q e r s

d t g c n h y

b j u o k

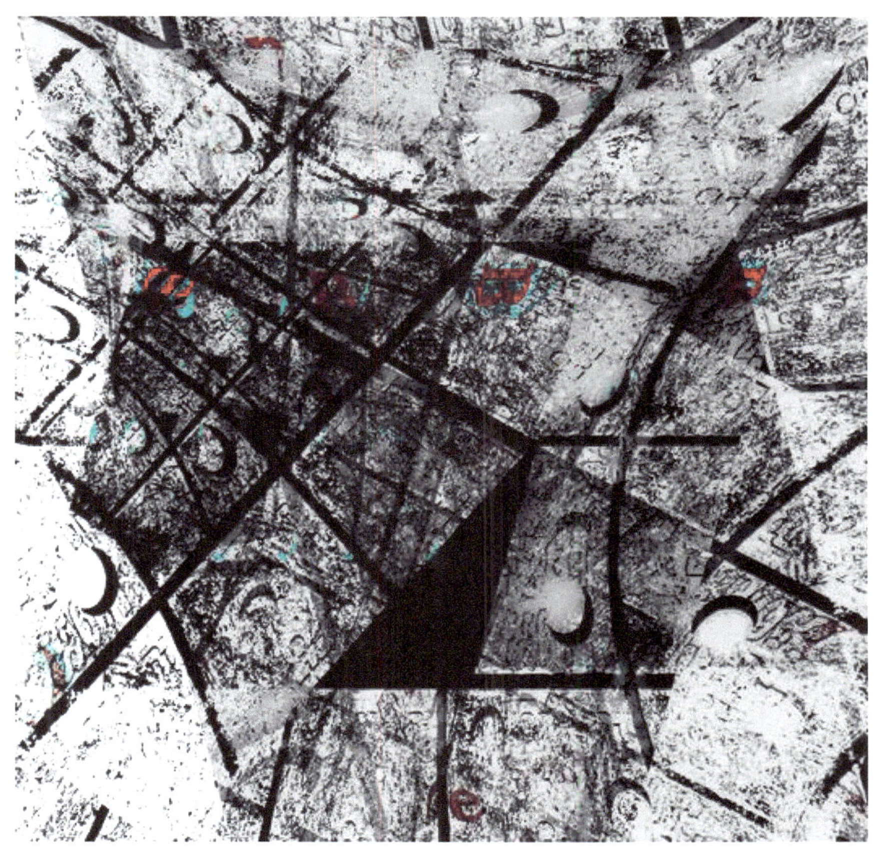

haiu-qt seared #30

jempo
xOxyerr
belat

haiu-qt seared #29

b o w t a

p e r y a h a

Z o T w e

haiu-qt seared #28

) y 6 7 o

G f a m t o t

r m (r –

XX

haiu-qt seared #27

- r (m r
s x t) f r s
r m (r –

haiu-qt seared #26

! F d s m
X t u w q " 5
z c f t n

haiu-qt seared #25

3 3 3 3 3
4 4 4 4 4 4 5
5 5 5 6 5

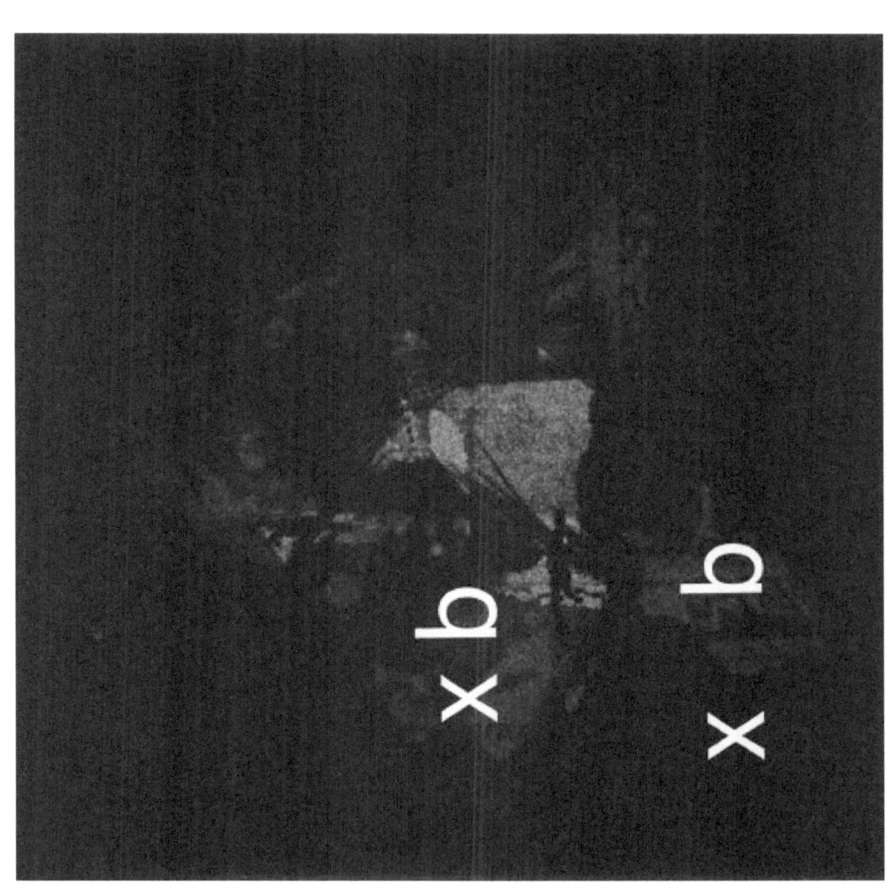

haiu-qt seared #24

1 1 1 1 1

2 2 2 2 2 2 2

11 1 11

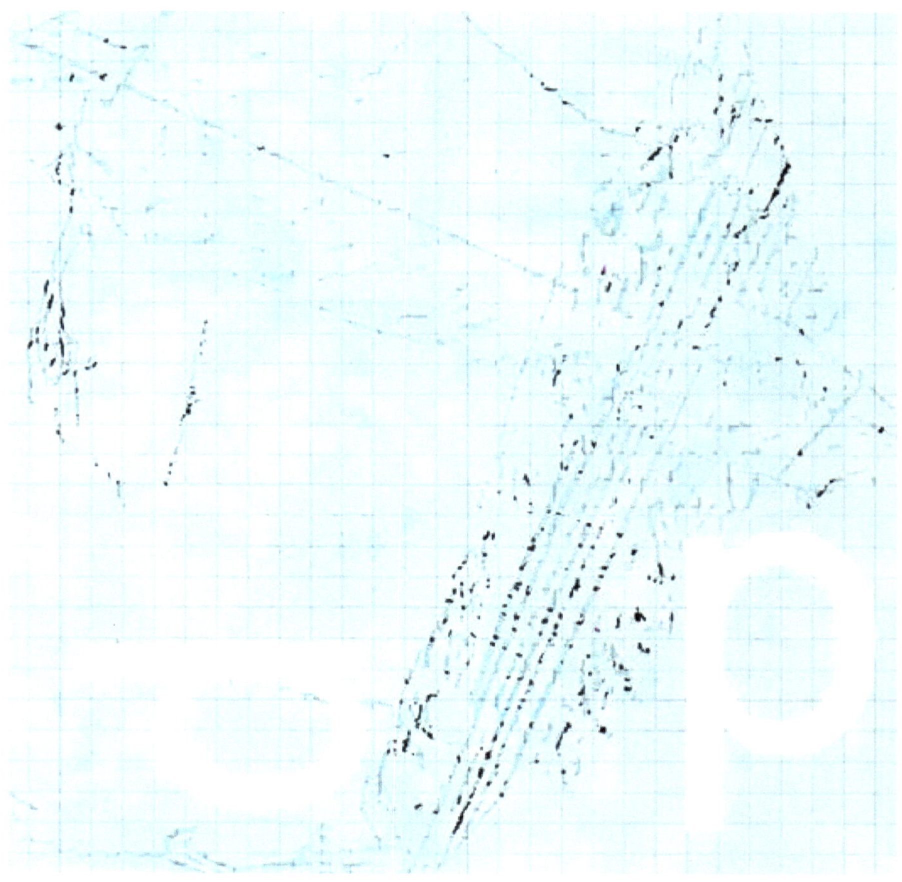

haiu-qt seared #45

5 s e M P
- \\ d b \\ h n
6 t f N Q

F

haiu-qt seared #46

p i o a t
a > + 3 s c r
o j p b s

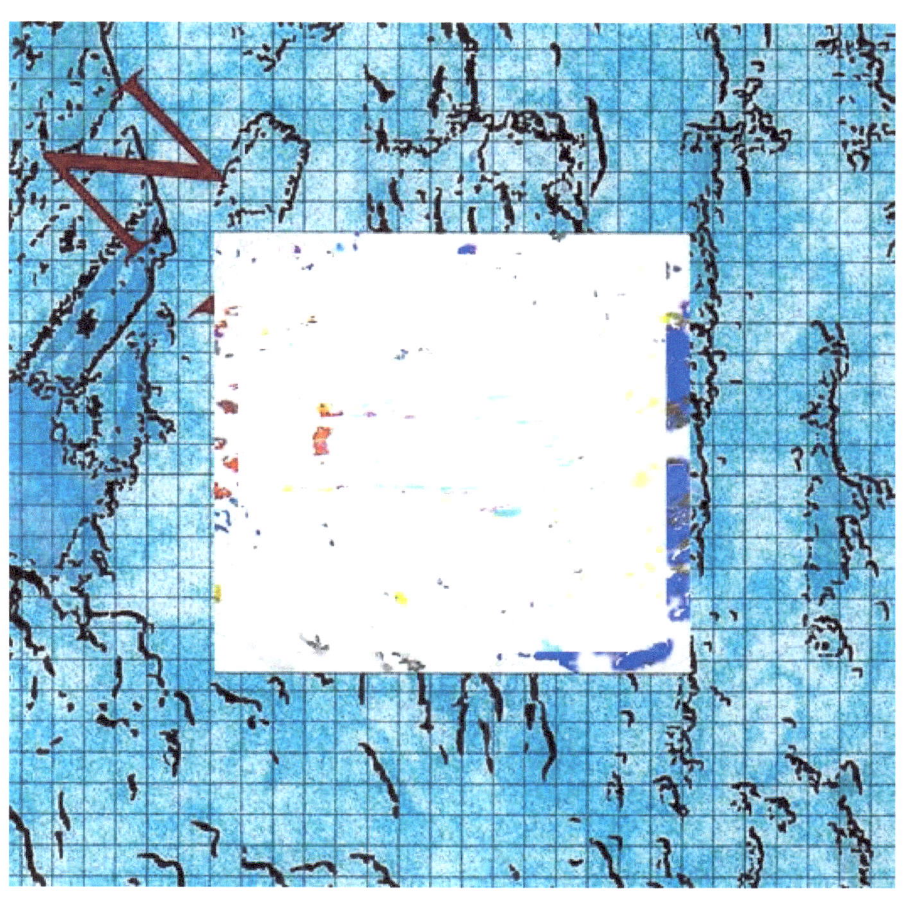

haiu-qt seared #47

c k h c k
[o m l r t]
d l i s l

haiu-qt seared #48

c q o y m
] : [p R b s
d r p x n

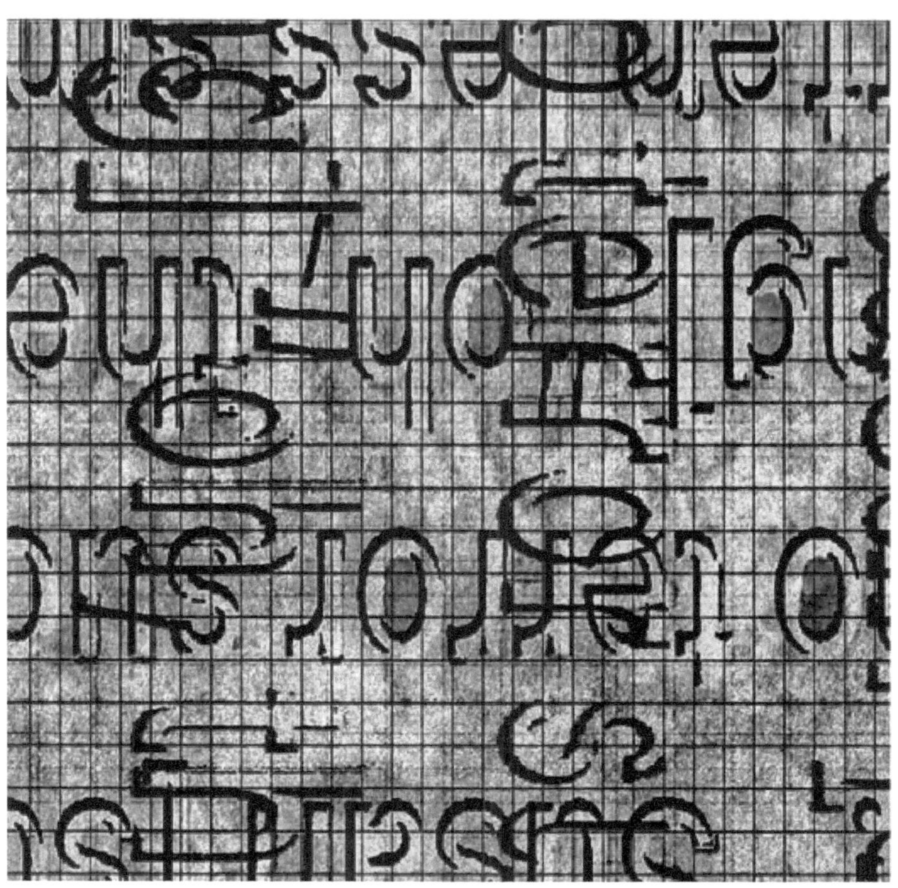

haiu-qt seared #49

m V q u t
w " • g p n t
n X r v s

harry k stammer is a writer, musician and painter who lives and works in Santa Barbara, CA USA. His books include *every beyond't nothing* (persistencia), *tents* (Otoliths), *grounds* (Otoliths); and *tocsin* (Otoliths), *sidewalkss* (Concrete Mist Press), *walls't's* (Sandy Press), -*48* (Sandy Press), *alleys't'* (Concrete Mist Press), *gravel* with Mark Young and Mark Cunningham and *gutter 's* (Sandy Press). Recent noise/poetry pieces are available at http://harrykstammer.bandcamp.com